WHEN KANGAROO GOES TO SCHOOL

BY **SONIA LEVITIN**   ILLUSTRATED BY **JEFF SEAVER**

rising moon

www.northlandpub.com

The illustrations were created using a
6x0 Rotring technical pen and colored pencils on plate finish 2-ply Bristol board.
Work in progress was converted to digital format and finished using Adobe graphics software
on an Apple Macintosh G4 equipped with a Wacom drawing tablet.
The text type was set in Zipty Do.
The display type was set in Spumoni L.P.
Composed in the United States of America

Printed in Hong Kong

FIRST IMPRESSION

01 02 03 04 05   5 4 3 2 1

Library of Congress Cataloging-in-Publication Data
Levitin, Sonia
When Kangaroo goes to school / Sonia Levitin ; illustrated by Jeff Seaver.
p.   cm.
Summary: Kangaroo learns the proper way to behave on the first day of school.
ISBN 0-87358-791-x
[1. Kangaroos—Fiction. 2. Etiquette—Fiction. 3. First day of school—Fiction. 4. Schools—Fiction.] I. Seaver, Jeff, ill. II. Title.
PZ7.L58 Wg 2001
[E]—dc21   2001019027

When you take Kangaroo to school, it helps to be prepared. The first day of school Kangaroo hops up and down, ready to run out the door. She is excited. Tell her, "Wait, Kangaroo! Are you ready for school? Do you know the rules?" School is more fun when you know what to expect. Now, help Kangaroo get ready.

Kangaroo will need new supplies for school. What kinds of supplies will she need? Crayons and markers, pencils and a pencil box, a glue stick, an eraser. Help Kangaroo put her new supplies into her backpack.

Of course, Kangaroo will want to take something to school for "show and tell." Everyone likes to take something to share. But some things do not belong there and must be left at home. Help Kangaroo decide what to take for "show and tell." What kinds of toys do not belong at school? Does Kangaroo know?

Kangaroo might wonder what to do when she gets hungry at school. Where will she eat? Kangaroo can take her lunch from home, or she can buy lunch in the cafeteria at school. Kangaroo may also want to take a snack. Help Kangaroo pack it in a sack.

Kangaroo will need to wash her face and comb her hair.
At home, Kangaroo loves to play in the dirt, but for school
it's best to be seen looking neat and clean.

If Kangaroo is walking to school, she should not leap over cars or reach up to the stars. She must step carefully and look both ways before crossing. Remind Kangaroo not to talk to strangers or to go anywhere with people she does not know. Crossing Guard is a friend indeed and will help Kangaroo cross the street.

If Kangaroo rides the bus to school, she must sit still until the
end of the line. Kangaroo must not hop or leap or climb.
Loud songs, whistles, and noises do not belong on the bus.

Kangaroo won't make a fuss if she takes a toy or a book along. She can softly hum a song or find new friends and talk about many things. The ride will seem short.

At school a monitor will help Kangaroo find her room. It has a number on the door. This is her class, where she will stay every day. Here she will study and learn and play.

In the classroom there might be a special desk or table for Kangaroo. The desk is hers, but not forever. She should not scratch her name on it with her claws because next year Elephant or Crocodile might use that desk.

When Teacher is talking, everyone should listen. Kangaroo
might rather hop or box or chew her socks. But Kangaroo must pay
attention. Sometimes Teacher will ask for questions or answers.
Then Kangaroo should raise her paw, without yelling "Ooo! Ooo!
I know, pick me!" Sometimes Teacher will call on Kangaroo.
Sometimes not.

Kangaroo will learn to read. She will be able to read stories and
poems and jokes. Reading is fun! First Kangaroo must learn the
alphabet. Does Kangaroo know the alphabet song? Do you?

At school Kangaroo will learn how to write. She will write her own name. She can write stories, letters, invitations, and signs. Some day she will write using the computer. She may even go on the internet and surf the Web! Kangaroo can send E-mail to her friends in Australia.

At school Kangaroo will learn arithmetic—how to count and measure. Then she can count her change when she goes to the store. By measuring, Kangaroo can make many things, like boxes, triangles, circles, and rings. Help Kangaroo to measure herself. How tall is Kangaroo?

Some things will be easy for Kangaroo to learn. Other lessons may take more time. Kangaroo can play games to help her practice reading and spelling and counting. Kangaroo likes to play hopscotch and jump rope. She can count the squares. She might sing songs while she jumps. Counting and singing are good ways to learn.

At lunch time, Teacher will take the class to the cafeteria. The cafeteria at school does not serve grass and acacia leaves. These are Kangaroo's favorites.

Ask her to try a taco for a change or a nice green salad.
She will need some money to pay for the food. Where did
Kangaroo put her lunch money? In
her pouch, that's where!

Kangaroo will love recess and play time. At play time, she can paint at the easel and help clean up the mess. There is a housekeeping corner, a reading corner, and even a "time out" corner. When Kangaroo forgets the rules, she will take "time out" to remember.

At recess time, Kangaroo should line up and wait her turn for the jungle gym. Kangaroo is the best at kick ball and climbing. She can balance on her tail. Everyone will clap and cheer, and Kangaroo will smile and say, "Thank you!" She might teach others to do tricks on the bar. That is how to make friends.

What if Kangaroo needs to go to the bathroom? She should raise her paw and ask for permission to leave. Or she may go to the teacher's desk and speak softly. Teacher will tell Kangaroo where to find the bathroom. When Kangaroo is finished using the bathroom, she should wash her paws, then come right back to class. She doesn't want to miss anything!

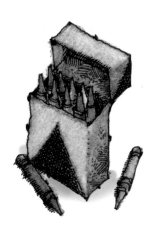

Kangaroo will listen closely when Teacher explains all the rules. Rules help everyone get along and stay safe. Bells ring at school to tell everyone when to start recess, when to come inside, or when there is an emergency.

Teacher will explain what to do in an emergency. *Hurry outside! Stay indoors! Get under your desk!* Sometimes there will be a fire drill. Kangaroo must hurry to do exactly what the teacher says. If everyone stays calm, there will be no harm.

One day there will be an "open house" at school. Teacher will talk about Kangaroo's work and play, how she gets along, and how she spends her day.

You will be proud when Teacher tells you how much Kangaroo has learned. Maybe Teacher will say this is the smartest kangaroo in the class. And probably she is.

kangaroo

Star Student

SONIA LEVITIN has written over thirty-five books and received many awards including the National Jewish Book Award, the Edgar Best Mystery Award, the Pen Award, and the Sydney Taylor Award.

NINE FOR CALIFORNIA, one of her popular picture books in the AMANDA SERIES, was a finalist for the California Young Reader Medal.

Ms. Levitin lives with her husband in Southern California and teaches Creative Writing at UCLA Extension. Her two dogs, Kinia and Isabella, have gone to school, of course. They bring in the morning newspapers and love to carry packages.

JEFF SEAVER has been a freelance illustrator for the past 26 years. Originally an architecture student, he is self-taught as an illustrator and has received numerous awards for his work. His clients have included major magazines, advertising agencies, book publishers, and Fortune 500 companies.

A long-time resident of New York City, Mr. Seaver recently migrated to the Connecticut shore where he lives with his daughter, Elizabeth, and several eccentric cats.